If You Give a Pig a Pancake

Once again, for Stephen —F.B.
For Laura Geringer, with love and eternal gratitude —L.N.

If You Give a

If You Give a Pig a Pancake
Text copyright © 1998 by Laura Numeroff
Illustrations copyright © 1998 by Felicia Bond
Manufactured in China. All rights reserved.
www.harpercollinschildrens.com

Library of Congress Cataloging-in-Publication Data
Numeroff, Laura Joffe.
  If you give a pig a pancake / by Laura Numeroff ; illustrated by Felicia Bond.
    p.   cm.
"A Laura Geringer Book"
  Summary: One thing leads to another when you give a pig a pancake.
  ISBN-10: 0-06-134955-0 — ISBN-13: 978-0-06-134955-3
  [1. Pigs—Fiction.]   I. Bond, Felicia, ill.   II. Title.
PZ7.N9641h   1998   97-36832
[E]—DC21   CIP
                                                                          AC

is a registered trademark of HarperCollins Publishers

Pig a Pancake

BY Laura Numeroff

ILLUSTRATED BY Felicia Bond

A Laura Geringer Book
An Imprint of HarperCollins*Publishers*

If you give a pig a pancake,

she'll want some syrup to go with it.

You'll give her some of your
favorite maple syrup.

She'll probably get all sticky,

so she'll want to take a bath.

She'll ask you for
some bubbles.

When you give her the bubbles,
she'll probably ask you for a toy.
You'll have to find your rubber duck.

The duck will remind her of the farm where she was born.
She might feel homesick and want to visit her family.

She'll want you to come too.
She'll look through your closet
for a suitcase.

Then she'll look under your bed.

When she's under the bed,
she'll find your old tap shoes.

She'll try them on. She'll probably
need something special to
wear with them.

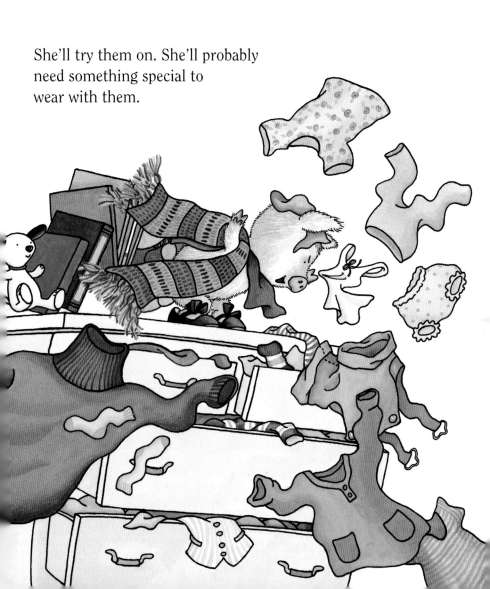

When she's all dressed, she'll ask for some music.

You'll play your
very best piano piece,
and she'll start dancing.

Then she'll want you to take her picture.

So you'll have to get your camera.

When she sees the picture,

she'll ask you to take more.

Then she'll want to send one to each of her friends.

You'll have to give her
some envelopes and stamps

and take her to the mailbox.

On the way, she'll see the tree in your backyard.
She'll want to build a tree house.

So you'll have to get her some wood,
a hammer, and some nails.

When the tree house is finished,

she'll want to decorate it.

She'll ask for wallpaper and glue.

When she hangs the wallpaper,
she'll get all sticky.

Feeling sticky will remind her
of your favorite maple syrup.

She'll probably ask you for some.

And chances are,

if she asks you for some syrup,

she'll want a pancake to go with it.